EAGLE AND NARWHAL'S INCREDIBLE ADVENTURES

Charles Harold Greene

CONTENTS

Dedication i

DEDICATION

This book is dedicated to Owen, Alexis, and Stephanie, with love and gratitude. For the time well spent, the lessons learned, and the moments of laughter.

Chapter One
The Whizenhunnt

Narwhal had heard that there are incredibly tall mountains in the heavens above his watery world. As a whale, he couldn't imagine how there were whole worlds above him and he wanted to see for himself.

So he pointed his unicorn nose upward and swam to the surface to take a look. He came so close to the shore that he could see people on the beach, and behind them the big mountains. He was sad though. No matter how hard he jumped out of the water, he kept on falling back in, and never got any closer to those mountains.

Suddenly an eagle flew down and said, "Whatcha doin?"

Narwhal said, "I want to go up to see the mountains. To see what they look like close up, but I can't."

"I'll make you a deal!" said Eagle. "I'll take you up to the top of mighty Mount Everest, the tallest of them all, if you take me under the ocean to see your mountains. My dad told me that islands are the tops of mountains. They just look like islands to me and I've always wanted to see for myself."

Narwhal agreed, and so Eagle took Narwhal's unicorn nose in his mighty talons, and flapped his mighty wings; Narwhal flapped his tail, and with a mighty team effort they flew up, up, and around, until they were in the clouds, and the snow and the wind howled and beat against them, right up to the top of Mount Everest.

It was amazing! But Narwhal was cold and Eagle was tired, so they started back down to the ocean. Finally they could see the ocean up ahead, but Eagle didn't think he could make it. Narwhal's tail was skimming the tops of trees. They were going to crash!

Fortunately though, Tiger saw that they were in trouble, and being a quick thinker, he leapt up through the branches and gave a push up on Narwhal's belly so that Eagle was able to land safely in the water with a big splash.

They quickly realized that Eagle wouldn't be able to go underwater long enough to see the underwater mountains.

"That's no fair!" said Eagle. "You promised, and I did my part of the deal!"

"I'm sorry!" cried Narwhal. "I didn't know you couldn't stay under water!"

"Do I look like a fish!? Now because you didn't think, I'll miss out on all that fun!"

In the middle of the argument, a turtle's head popped out of the water. After watching for a few moments, he yelled to get their attention.

"Hey! Uuh... hi!" said the turtle. Eagle and Narwhal looked up in surprise. "My Grandpa told me that the only way to win an argument is to be the first to drop it," he continued.

"That doesn't make any sense!" said Eagle. "I don't believe it!"

"Well it's true," said Turtle. "He said when someone's mad and arguing, there's no way to change their mind because they're so focused on trying to change yours."

"That kind of makes sense," said Narwhal. "Plus, I don't see how arguing is going to help me take you underwater."

"If you could do that, you could make pigs fly too I bet!" laughed Turtle. "You told Eagle you would bring him down for a visit?"

"Ya, but I didn't know he couldn't stay under water. I think he'd like to see The Coral Ridges," said Narwhal. "I just wanted to show him where we live." Narwhal looked sad.

Eagle felt bad for being upset. He still wanted to see the underwater world though. "It's okay Narwhal," he said. "I didn't think about it either. Do you know of any way I can get down there?" he asked Turtle.

Turtle said, "If anyone can help, it's a Whizenhunnt. They're super scary, but they know a lot of stuff. I think one lives out by that island. I'll see if I can find her, then meet you out there."

So Eagle took to the air, and Narwhal charged through the water. Together they raced off for the island. When they got there, they had to wait a long time. Eagle was getting tired of sitting around, but Turtle arrived finally.

"I'm now going to introduce you to the Whizenhunnt," said Turtle. "But don't worry, she's a lot scarier than she looks."

Eagle was nervous but he didn't know why. Narwhal was nervous too. He had never seen a Whizenhunnt and it made him jittery being this close to one in the water. If only he could fly like Eagle.

Suddenly, behind Turtle, a shiny black shape with a pointy top rose out of the water, followed by two large watery eyes that peered out from beneath a wide wobbly rim that went all the way around the head. The rest of the creature stayed out of sight under the water.

"Okay," said Turtle. "Tell her what you need."

Eagle whispered to Narwhal, "You tell her! I'm scared!"

Narwhal whispered to Eagle, "No! You tell her! I'm scared too!"

"Okay, Okay!" said Eagle, ruffling his feather and trying to look brave. He looked at the two eyes under the wobbly rim, and told them that he wanted to see the underwater world but he didn't know how, and was wondering if she might be able to help.

The big glossy eyes looked at him closely for a moment, narrowed, and then slid beneath the surface. A long tentacle-like finger reached up and tapped Turtle on the head, beckoning him below.

After some minutes Turtle reappeared. "Okay Eagle. She said you have to jump into the water, close your eyes, and sink towards the bottom. She'll take care of the rest. Just trust her. And it's really important that you stay relaxed. She said especially to tell you that."

"That's crazy!" cried Eagle. "What if she eats me?" Narwhal and Turtle agreed that it was a risk, but Turtle was fairly certain Whizenhunnts didn't eat animals with feathers. Eagle really wanted to see the underwater world, and after some discussion, he agreed. So flying up into the air, he relaxed into a roll, took a deep breath, and dove head first into the water.

"Relax, Relax, Relax," he kept saying as he sunk deeper into the dark cold water. It was too late to turn back now. He wasn't that great a swimmer, and he was almost out of breath. His heart thundered in his ears. His lungs felt like they were going to explode... and then he saw her! A huge octopus type creature with a pointy black hat, huge bulbous eyes, a large warty nose, and no mouth.

He screamed out a stream of bubbly terror. He was cloaked in water, sinking fast, and not at all relaxed. The Whisenhunnt swam around him in circles. She

shot out a great cloud of jet black ink from the end of one of her tentacles; it surrounded him like a cloak. Everything went dark. Eagle was losing consciousness. Suddenly, the ink collapsed against his feathers, squeezing like a tight hand, then exploded out into a great bubble, surrounding him. He was completely dry and flying inside a bubble of air.

He drew in great, heaving breaths, hardly believing he was alive. There was Narwhal swimming behind the Whizenhunnt, and Turtle too. Other than that, all around, up and down, it was water, water, water, and a blurry, faint, bottom of the sea drifting away into the darkness.

The Whizenhunnt swam up close to the bubble, her many tentacles writhing, her great bulbous eyes staring at him. Eagle whimpered and tried to fly away from her, but the bubble was only so big and he was trapped. "So much for trust and relaxation," he thought. "This is where I become supper."

"I'm not going to eat you," said the Whizenhunnt. Her voice was faint and hollow sounding inside the bubble.

"EEEAKE! She can read my mind!" The Whizenhunnt laughed. She definitely didn't have a mouth. "This is just too much for a poor eagle!" cried Eagle. "I wish I were back in the real world and never wanted to explore the ocean!"

"That may be," said the Whizenhunnt with her hollow voice. "but you're here now, and there's no time to argue. You have two choices. One, you can trust me, and continue this watery journey; or two, you can resist your present reality, your bubble will burst, and you will be lost in the blackness of your resistance."

"Not much of a choice there!" cried Eagle, not knowing what the 'blackness of his resistance' was. "I'll go with the first option!"

"Good choice!" said the Whizenhunnt. "This is where you really need to relax and pay attention. If you flap around and freak out, this won't work. I've never actually done it before."

"Great!" said Eagle, "That really helps me relax!"

"Just do as I say and you'll probably be okay."

"Probably!?" cried Eagle.

"Now be quiet and listen! You have everything you need in your own mind. Do as I say... Close your eyes... Take slow deep breaths... Forget the past... and forget the future... Forget everything but now… Forget everything but the flowing of the currents."

So he did.

༄༄༄༄༄༄

Narwhal and Turtle knew about a lot of things, but Eagles and Whizenhunnts were mostly new to them. They watched from a short distance, not understanding what was going on, and quite a bit scared. They could see Eagle flying around in a huge air bubble. The Whizenhunnt was swimming around the bubble, tentacles treading water, her funny pointed hat floating in the current like a cone shaped jellyfish. Eagle's eyes were almost as big as hers. The Whizenhunnt was talking softly and earnestly. Once, Eagle wailed that he wished he were back in the real world. Then he closed his eyes, and the Whizenhunnt stretched her eight long arms around the bubble, closing her eyes too, and the bubble slowly collapsed until it was shaped to his body like a shimmering suit of air.

"Grandpa's never going to believe this!" whispered Turtle.

The Whizenhunnt pushed the bubble in here, pulled it out there until it was a perfect fit. She opened her eyes and smiled with her mouthless face.

"You can open your eyes now." said the Whizenhunnt. "Your suit is made of air. It's easily damaged, but l can teach you to maintain and strengthen it with the power of your mind." She seemed quite pleased with herself.

Eagle was so excited when he saw his shiny new suit that he didn't hear anything she was saying. He was able to fly! Under water! It was incredible! It was shimmery and it made him feel lighter than air. It wasn't at all like flying up in the real world. It was like being weightless; effortlessly afloat. Just floating on his back like a bad mama jama, with an awesome super suit, looking super cool!

"Oh yeah!" he screamed, "Look at me now! Have you ever seen anything as awesome as this before!?"

Narwhal and Turtle looked at one another in surprise as they watched Eagle trying out his new duds. He was really fast. He was doing flips and cartwheels

and kicking dives, his talons extended in a wild blur, screaming out whoops and hollers and acrobatics.

"Oh goodness," said Turtle, "I hope he's not headed for... yep, he is. Grandpa always says it's smart to look before you swim. I guess Eagle didn't know that..."

Narwhal was off like a flash, screaming at the top of his lungs, "Eagle! Eagle! Stoppppp! Come back! You're headed right for the kelp fields! Pull up! Pull up!"

But Eagle was going so fast that he didn't hear. He was making a beautiful roundhouse sweeping kick move, and before he knew what was happening, his wings were all tangled in long, dark, slimy ropes. They wrapped around his body as quickly as he had dashed among them; binding him and dragging him down to the bottom where he disappeared into the deep shadows.

"Help Me!" Eagle screamed. "I'm down here! Help! Help!"

The kelp seemed to suck him to the bottom. "Help!" he screamed over and over, struggling against the kelp. His air suit was in shreds. Small portions clung to his body. A small bubble remained about around his head. His breath was coming in small sharp gasps. He stopped screaming and looked around him.

It was dark. He could see Narwhal's silhouette swimming in circles above him. From up there he would look like a patch of sand beneath the kelp, and Narwhal wouldn't be able to see him.

Then he realized he was surrounded by crabs. Great big ones displaying hungry pinchers. Lurking behind the crabs were giant eels longer than his wingspan with hungry, patient eyes. The crab's claws clacked musically as they made scuttling attacks, and quickly retreated.

Eagle was desperate. The bubble around his head was getting smaller and his waterlogged wings were coiled in a mass of weeds and feathers. With one last desperate effort, he grasped one of his heavy wing feathers in his talons and painfully tore it out, then stretching his leg as high as he could, he let it go. The looping current grabbed the feather up like a wind-swept leaf falling from an autumn maple tree. It swept up, swirling, swirling, and blew right past Narwhal's unicorn nose, catching his eye.

"Eagle!" he screamed, and watched as the current turned in upon itself, bringing the feather back down to where it had started. Narwhal saw Eagle. And he saw how much trouble he was in too.

Keeping a sharp eye on Eagle, he yelled to Turtle, "Go get the Whizenhunnt! Quick! I see Eagle and I'm going down to help him! He's in trouble!"

With that, he dove towards the bottom, attacking the crabs with his unicorn nose. A big one had just been going for Eagles head bubble, but Narwhal blocked him at the last moment, sweeping three more away with his tail on his first pass. It didn't take long to fight the crabs off, and the eels were gone at the first sign of danger.

When the crabs were scattered, Narwhal said, "Stay calm buddy! Try not to breathe heavy! Turtle is going for help." He worked carefully to disentangle Eagle's feathers from the kelp. "Stay still! Let me do it!"

Eagle was so frightened. With every breath he could feel the bubble fluttering against his cheeks. If only he had listened to the Whizenhunnt before his wild and crazy test drive! He promised himself that he would never! never! never! show off in front of Narwhal or Turtle again! And thank goodness for Narwhal! he thought. He couldn't really talk right now, but when he could he was going to tell Narwhal thank you.

Eagle was so happy when he saw Turtle diving down into the kelp just behind the Whizenhunnt. He might make it after all! His vision was going blurry, but before he lost consciousness, he saw a cloud of black ink shooting from the end of a long suction cuppy leg. He was being squeezed by a strong hand, and then he was inside a bubble, gasping in full deep breaths of cool moist air. He coughed, and gasped, and coughed, flapping his wings. Feathers dropped and floated around him like snow in a snow globe. Every part of him hurt. His head was pounding. His wing was stinging where he had pulled out the feather. The pressure inside his beak made him want to scream. But he was alive!

When he finally got his breath and composure back, he said, "Wow... Sorry guys. Um... I guess I should be more careful." He was too shaken to be embarrassed.

"Well it's true," said Turtle, "You don't listen very well. My grandpa— "

"No, it's okay," said Narwhal. "I'm just glad you're okay. That was an awesome show you put on! I've never seen anybody go so fast! You must have been going— "

"I know!" said Turtle. "Superfast! Like a superfast out of control Marlin straight into the kelp! I've never seen a Marlin move like that though. You did a bunch of crazy flips and dives and kicks."

Eagle was already feeling better about his near-death experience. "I know right!? I was like, Ka-Chau, and Hyyaaa, and Cheeeehaya!" His flips and twirls were getting bigger and faster as his re-enactment ramped-up.

Suddenly Eagle felt his bubble being jerked hard left out of a Beautifully Graceful Backwards Swan Dive Ninja Kick Move, and found himself face-to-face with the Whizenhunnt.

"I think there's someone you forgot to thank!"

Eagle was too scared to say anything at all. He just stared into those large squishy eyes.

"In fact you forgot to say thank you TWICE now! What do you expect from a Feathered Upper Worlder I guess." She spun Eagle like a top in the water and then grabbed him again face-to-face. She said nothing for a long squint-eyed minute, then, "They're usually worthless." she muttered, as if to herself.

"Hey, I'm sorry!" cried Eagle. "I wasn't thinking! Thank you for saving me! And I'm not worthless!"

"That may be true," said the Whizenhunnt. "Not yet anyways. Not if you can learn to be still long enough to listen, and think before you act. You could even become something great." The Whizenhunnt look sideways at Narwhal and Turtle. "You two! Pay attention here! This won't hurt you to know."

They nodded and moved in a little closer on the other side of Eagle.

"Now listen Eagle," continued the Whizenhunnt. "When your mind is jumping about like the waves on the surface, your air suit is going to be fragile. That's why the soft kelp was able to tear it up. But if your mind is strong and steady like the deep currents, like a deep slow breath, the waves on the surface won't bother it, and your suit will be strong. This is your first lesson."

Eagle was confused. Narwhal was confused too.

"That sounds a lot like the stuff Grandpa talks about," said Turtle, "when I sit with him beneath the Coral Tree. Sometimes we take a nap." The Whizenhunnt looked at Turtle.

"Excuse me," said Eagle, "You said something about deep currents?"

"I was talking about your busy little mind. You need to slow it down. Give it some space so it can see. Without a strong mind you'll never survive down here."

"Oh goodness!" said Eagle. "I don't know if I'm cut out for this!"

"You're not!" cried the Whizenhunnt. "You're a sack of feathers! I don't know why you're here, but you've got a flier's pair of strong lungs and it's time you start using them!"

"I'm so confused!" said Eagle.

"My grandpa talks about breathing sometimes, usually right before a nap." said Turtle.

"Yes, breathing," said the Whizenhunnt. "You need to clear your mind. That's all. Just look at your breath in your mind instead of thinking." Whizenhunnt shook her head. "This is hopeless," she said. "Okay Eagle, let's practice. Do exactly as I say. Close your eyes."

Eagle closed his eyes.

"You too, you two!" said the Whizenhunnt sharply to Narwhal and Turtle.

They squeezed their eyes tightly shut.

Whizenhunnt continued, "Now clear your mind and forget everything but the flowing of the currents. Just try it."

Eagle quickly started hyperventilating. Narwhal kept his eyes screwed tightly shut and held his breath, hoping the Whizenhunnt wouldn't see him despite his twelve foot bulk. Turtle rolled peacefully onto his back, and floating in the current, closed his eyes and took a nap.

"Stop it, stop it!" said the Whizenhunnt to Eagle. "You're trying to calm down, not black out… This is hopeless! Wake that Turtle up!"

Narwhal, being closest to Turtle, nudged him and whispered loudly, "Turtle! Turtle! Wake up! She wants to talk to you. Pssst! Wake up!"

Turtle rolled slowly onto his stomach, blinking his eyes. "Hmmm? Wha..?" He said.

"The Whizenhunnt," mouthed Narwhal, rolling his eyes in her direction.

"Wakey wakey, Turtle," said the Whizenhunnt. "I need to ask you a question. You said your grandpa naps beneath a coral tree. What's his name?"

"Papa Numa," said Turtle. "That's what everyone calls him, but I call him Grandpa."

"Interesting," said the Whizenhunnt. "Very interesting indeed. Can you take us to him?"

"Sure," said Turtle. "Follow me."

જાજાજાજાજાજી

So they all swam off following Turtle, Eagle still unsteady on his wings. His new air suit made moving so effortless that it was hard to control his speed.

They swam out over the kelp fields towards deeper water; over a deep black hole where the ground dropped away into the vast depths. Eagle felt disoriented. He couldn't see anything to get his bearings on. When he was flying around in The Upper World, he could always see the ground, and could tell where he was. After a long time, the ground rose slowly up from the depths. Faint at first, but then gathering detail as it came up to meet them. Eagle was feeling better now. Everything was so strange here. It was quieter, and he felt so light.

Up ahead there were obvious signs of life. "This is where Papa Numa lives," said Turtle, pointing to a tidy but simple dwelling. "And that's his Coral Tree over there," he said, pointing behind, and just over the hill to where they could see the tops of the beautiful corals swaying gently in the current. "I bet he's down there right now. I'll go get him."

"No, no!" said the Whizenhunnt. "We'll wait here until he's done napping and then you can introduce us. In fact, why don't you three go get some food. I bet you're hungry."

Now that she mentioned it, "Yeah, super hungry!"

So Eagle, Narwhal, and Turtle went off for a nice meal of sea cucumbers. Then Turtle showed them around the village. After that, Eagle decided he was tired and had better take a nap, too. In fact, he was so tired he slept all day. Flying up around Mt Everest, and then all the underwater excitement had really worn him out. During his long nap, he became somewhat of a celebrity; the Feathered Upper Worlder sleeping in Papa Numa's bed. Quite a stir it caused.

The Whizenhunnt and Papa Numa spent a great deal of time talking, and napping too. When Eagle woke up he was groggy and disoriented, but super hungry. He dug right into some more cucumbers.

The Whizenhunnt came in while he was eating. "Alive I see. Well, as soon as you're done with that cucumber I'll introduce you to Papa Numa." Eagle nodded his head okay, and quickly finished. He followed her down the hill to the Coral Tree. The Whizenhunnt sat down and motioned for Eagle to sit down too.

Eagle sat expectantly, but after a few long moments, Papa Numa still hadn't moved and his eyes were closed. Eagle started to say something, but the Whizenhunnt waggled a tentacle at him, and he closed his beak. Papa Numa sat with his back against the tree breathing deep, even breaths. Eagle wasn't a good judge of turtles' ages, but he could tell this one was really really old. After a long time Papa Numa opened his eyes and looked at Eagle. "Hi Eagle," he said.

"Hi," Eagle said. "They told me you were going to help me learn how to use this suit."

Papa Numa smiled, "I don't know much about your suit, but there's a small chance I'll be able to help you in some way." He closed his eyes.

Eagle looked at the Whizenhunnt and raised his eyebrows. She lowered her eyebrows threateningly and waggled a tentacle at him. He shrugged his shoulders and stayed quiet. 'I wonder what Narwhal and Turtle are up to,' he wondered. 'Probably off playing games and joking around somewhere.'

Eagle didn't know that Turtle had swam up and was sitting behind him until Papa Numa said, "Hi Turtle. How are you today?" Papa Numa hadn't opened his eyes.

"I'm good, Grandpa," said Turtle. "I was just talking to the Beverly Brothers. They said their pa saw more white creeping in on the lower ridges. They said Mrs. Wynnieston said it must have something to do with Eagle. She wants to talk to him."

"I see," said Papa Numa. "I'll assure her that Eagle isn't responsible for the creeping white, a darker mystery than it's color suggests. As you can see, I'm just getting to know your feathered friend myself. I was going to tell him about our game. The one where I say, "Close your eyes and look at... and then you say

something like, 'your ear, or heart; or something outside of us, like friends or the coral tree'."

"Oh yeah," said Turtle. "That's a fun game. Eagle may not get it though."

"I don't get it," said Eagle. "How do you look at something with your eyes closed?"

"That's a good question," said Papa Numa. "Here's another one, Eagle. What do you want to do? Or maybe the question is, what are you looking for in this under world of water?"

Eagle thought about it for a minute, then said, "I want to explore, and go on adventures! I want to see new things! To learn the secrets of all the mysteries; and I want to be a hero too!" he said. "A guy with a super suit this awesome should be a super hero!"

"Awwwe, I see. Well, that's good," said Papa Numa. "We always need heroes."

Chapter Two
King Brighton

After what seemed like weeks and weeks of practicing his brain exercises with Papa Numa, Eagle was tired, but happy with himself. He'd made a lot of progress. His underwater flying ability was greatly improved, and he had more control over his air suit. It was so much stronger and more durable.

In between his long hours of training and exercise, Eagle played with Narwhal and Turtle. They went on long exploring excursions, and played with the other young ones in the village. He made friends with the Beverly Brothers, and Mrs. Wynnieston's granddaughter, Lucy. He even talked to Mrs Wynnieston, but he wasn't sure what she meant when she asked about the white coral. He was becoming well liked, both for the novelty of being a Feathered Upper Worlder, but also because he was nice.

One day when they were back from exploring, Papa Numa told them that news of the Upper Worlder living on The Coral Ridge had reached the imperial ears of King Brighton Partholon, and he expected the pleasure of this Eagle's attending him at lunch, on the morrow.

Narwhal and Turtle were ecstatic. "Can you believe it!" said Turtle. "We're going to see the King Brighton! I've heard Papa Numa talk about him, but I never thought I would see him myself!"

"It sounds exciting!" exclaimed Eagle. "What's a morrow? The king said he wants to have lunch on it."

Papa Numa chuckled. "That means that he's expecting us for lunch tomorrow. To... morrow."

Eagle was excited, but scared as much as anything, knowing that he would be the center of attention.

So… Early the next morning Papa Numa, the Whizenhunnt, Turtle, Eagle, and Narwhal, all left the village for the long swim around the Great Horn Reef, along The Abysmal Drop, through three different currents, and finally, just in time for lunch, they arrived at the magnificent palace of King Brighton Partholon.

Eagle was impressed. He had never seen anything so impressive in all his life, either above or below. The gate was guarded by massive walrus; their huge tusks glistening in the golden, shimmery light that emanated from the conch shells lining the pathway. The gates were made from massive pearls, and the most beautiful plants grew from every crack in the magnificent masonry making up the mighty walls. Inside it was decorated with statues of penguins. They lined the walls in every posture and attitude. Some declaiming to the skies. Some contemplating. Some holding the implements of war. Others stared directly at eagle; their eyes seemed to follow him.

All around him remarkable creatures hurried here and there. Seahorse and starfish held discussions in corners. There were marlin and jellyfish and octopus too; parrot-fish, clown fish, and even a shark. Eagle was followed by silence. All the creatures looked and whispered, pointed and stared.

"Look!" they said. "It's the Upper Worlder! How silky his feathers beneath his silvery suit of air! How effortlessly he slides through the water as if he hasn't a care!"

Eagle was shy and overwhelmed.

They came to a door behind which he knew they must find the king. It was guarded by even bigger walrus, with huger tusks, and voices so deep they felt like the rumble of a mountain. One brute swung the mighty doors open, and introduced to the court in a mighty voice, *"PAPA NUMA AND EAGLE OF THE UPPER WORLD... AND COMPANY!"* His voice was so big that it crashed in the confined space, creating vortices in the water.

In response came a voice built much more like a whistle, "Enter!" it shrilled out in commanding tones. Papa Numa gestured for them to follow him, and they all entered the throne room.

It was a beautiful room. Tall plants lined the walls which were built of colorful corals that swirled and twisted around one another until the enclosed space was a harmony of beauty and nature. It was a large space, but packed shoulder-to-

shoulder with a bewildering assortment of creatures. Most of them looked foreign to Eagle, but even Turtle and Narwhal were mystified by some of the remarkable characters present.

Through the crowd they went, up to the presentation platform, just below the dais where King Brighton sat upon his black agate throne. Eagle felt much better when he saw that the king wasn't much taller than himself, and had tiny wings. He took his bow between Papa Numa and Narwhal. Eagle hadn't known that penguins had small voices. At least King Brighton did. He asked Eagle all about his life. Where he came from. What it was like there. He walked around Eagle, looking him over very closely from all perspectives while talking. Apparently a lot of people had been speculating about him, and the King was looking for answers.

After a long discussion about pecking orders and politics in the feathered world, the king said, "So I hear you've got some fly moves. You're fast. Is it true?"

Eagle knew it wasn't bragging to admit the truth. "Yeah, I'm pretty fast," he said. "Still getting the hang of this underwater thing though. It can be a lot like riding a pogo stick on a bowling ball."

The king laughed. "I'll tell you what Mr. Feather!" he said "Come on out to The Gaming Grounds, and let's put on a little demonstration for the people. It's good to provide entertainment, you know. Keeps them quiet and sleepy," he added confidentially. "I'll have you race my fastest champion! That should be fun!"

ভ ভ ভ ভ ভ ভ

So Eagle and Papa Numa and Narwhal and Turtle and all the court followed King Brighton out to The Gaming Grounds. They could hear the booming voices of the walruses calling the people to *"The free entertainment provided by Good King Brighton, Here and Now, At The Gaming Grounds; Come One, Come All, For the King's Entertainment!"*

It was amazing how fast The Gaming Grounds filled up. The middle was a space where all kinds of spectacles could be presented, and was surrounded by

stadium seating. The king had a throne on a dais under a canopy with a megaphone on a hinged arm beside him. He said into it, "Okay my people, peeps, and friends! We're going to have a race! Starting in the red corner, The Magnificent Feathered Eagle of the Upper World! Oh Yeah! Can I get a cheer for that awesome bubble he's wearing! Aaaand his opponent, racing from the blue corner! Can I hear a big cheer for our one and only, ooooour well beloved! Suuuuper Fleeeeet, Our Favorite Silver Marlinnnnn, The Fastest Of My Fast Friends!"

The crowd went crazy screaming and cheering. Eagle was excited! His heart was pounding. The Marlin circled him looking fleet indeed. They lined up on the line, the line judge waved his flag, and they were off! The crowd went silent. Before Super Fleet was thirty feet from the starting line, Eagle was already at the end! Done and done!

Eagle did a little celebration jig. The crowd, after a moment of stunned silence, erupted in a standing ovation. It was deafening. You could barely hear the king screaming into his megaphone, "That was amazing! Go again! Go again! Go again!"

Again, Eagle was lined up next to Super Fleet. And again, Eagle was so fast it was just no competition. Eagle was feeling better and better. He did a couple more flips and jigs in celebration. The crowd went wild with oooh's and aaawe's. The king screamed excitedly into his megaphone, "Show us what you've got Eagle! Let's see your moves!"

So Eagle did a little demonstration. He streaked around The Gaming Grounds, just over the head of the spectators with loops and curls and twists and kicks. Then from one end of the track to the other, it was high speed ninja spin kicks, swooping death widows, and any number of high speed, mind-numbing twirls and flips. The crowd was loving it! Even Papa Numa and the Whizenhunnt were impressed. Narwhal and Turtle cheered right along with everyone. "Go Eagle! Go Eagle! Oh Yeah! That's it! You're my Eagle!"

Eagle was elated. The King was cheering, jumping up and down and clapping his flippers like a little penguin. Eagle had one more trick for them. He'd saved the best for last. It was a Reverse Upside-down Bilateral. In his mind it was all so slow and easy, but he was actually going super fast, and just as his feet cleared

his head, on the back side of the upward spin, his shoulders and head collided with the track, and he went bouncing and rolling all the way down until he skidded with a Thump! into the wall at the base of the king's dais, a crumpled mass of feathers and air suit.

Through the pain, Eagle felt an overwhelming sense of embarrassment. Then he saw the king's head peering over the ledge and down at him with a worried expression on his face. "That was some trick lad. You okay?"

Eagle was able to get up. He hurt everywhere. "Yes sir, I'm fine, thank you. I'm sure I'll be okay," he told the king, trying not to cry. It hurt bad, but the embarrassment hurt worse.

The rest of the day was an adventure even though he was limping. They had a big meal fit for a king. There was music, and entertainments that Eagle was able to watch instead of participate in, which was nice. The king insisted they spend the night. "Lots of extra bedrooms!" he exclaimed. Eagle got to sleep in the arms of a statue of Athena that had come down in a ship many years ago.

While Eagle slept, Papa Numa spent long hours talking with the king in a private study.

〜〜〜〜〜〜

The next morning, while it was still very early, Papa Numa woke Eagle, Narwhal, and Turtle, telling them it was time to head for home. Back through the three currents, past The Abysmal Drop, around the Great Horned Reef, and finally back to The Coral Ridge with Papa Numa's hut, and the Coral Tree where he likes to nap.

On the journey, Papa Numa asked Eagle what he thought about his day with the king. Eagle said that it had been fun, but he had been super embarrassed when he wiped out at The Gaming Grounds. Papa Numa told him that wiping out was nothing to be embarrassed about. "There's nothing wrong with messing up when you're trying to do the right thing, and you're doing your best. In fact," he said, "you should be happy you crashed."

"Every time you crash," continued Papa Numa, "you can use it to make yourself stronger and more capable. Your crash shows you where you need to practice. Crashing also helps us stay humble." he smiled. "It reminds us that we're not perfect, and shows that we have room to grow. That's something to be grateful for, because if there's room to grow, then there's more to know, and if there's more to know, then you're not done yet. How exciting is that? So you see, crashing was really a good thing."

That night while everyone was preparing to sleep, Papa Numa told Narwhal and Turtle that he needed their most attentive services the next day. They would have to get up early, so sleep hard and then have a good breakfast. He told Eagle the same thing, but that he would be spending the day with the Whizenhunnt, not something Eagle liked the sound of.

Early the next morning, Papa Numa went out with Narwhal and Turtle, and was gone for a while before coming back by himself. He wouldn't tell Eagle where Narwhal and Turtle were going.

"You just worry about keeping your mind clear and your thoughts quiet," said Papa Numa. "You're going to have a long day. It's time to advance your training to include high speed visual acuity through mental clarity. Think of it as high-speed seeing. Super vision. The foundation is in the mind, fulfillment through the body. You must become the synthesis of breath, velocity, and clear seeing." That's all sounded good to Eagle, especially if it helped him not embarrass himself again.

The Whizenhunnt arrived in a silent swirling swish of tentacles and glaring eyeballs. She made three snapping sounds, and Eagle knew it was time to go. He tried not to worry about what they were going to be doing all day. There's no reason to create stress when you don't even know what you should be stressing about, he told himself.

For a long time they swam away downhill into deeper, darker waters, past a few cloudy kelp beds, then out onto a flat surface all cut by jagged channels interlaced like a web. It looked as if the sea floor had cracked and shattered. There was no vegetation, no color, and no sign of life. The Whizenhunnt settled onto the ocean floor sending a swirling cloud of dust into the water.

"Papa Numa tells me your eyes aren't fast enough to slow things down yet. You need to see quicker."

"Isn't that a paradox?" asked Eagle.

"That depends on which direction you're looking from. It means you need to focus less on seeing, and more on creating the open mindscape to see with."

"Hold on, hold on!" said Eagle. "You're saying that if I want to see better, I need to focus less on seeing?"

"Yes, exactly. You need fewer thoughts in your head. If your mind is full of thoughts, then it's not paying any attention to seeing. Your thoughts are slowing you down, slowing your eyes down and telling them lies. Discard them from your head and create room for seeing what actually is. With enough practice, no matter how fast your body flies through the water, your mind will always arrive first to get a good look, and you'll already know what to do when you get there. The official term for this is Far Sighted Visual Acuity. It's very difficult to master."

"I think I see what you mean... but no... not really. Are you sure I don't see good enough already?"

"Not even close. Here's what we're going to do. Go off a little ways, about a hundred meters or so, then fly back past me as fast as you can. I'll throw a piece of kelp up into the current. You need to see it in time to cut it with your talons. Remember! A clear mind provides the extra mental space you need to see the truth without the cloudiness of preconceived judgments. Now fly your fastest! Go!"

'Is she serious!?' Eagle thought. 'As fast as I can? This is going to be hard!'

He swam off a ways and turned around. There was the Whizenhunnt. The light was so dim that she was just a gray silhouette against a deeper gloom. He was sure he wouldn't be able to see the kelp at all, let alone strike it accurately. It would be like trying to hit a golf ball with a baseball bat, from an airplane, at sunset.

'Okay! Here goes!' he thought. 'Clear your mind and let the kelp come to you!'

Off he shot like a rocket from an underwater rocket gun. He went past the Whizenhunnt so fast she spun around like a top in the eddies of his back current. It took him two hundred meters to get stopped! He hadn't seen the kelp.

"Start again from where you are!" yelled the Whizenhunnt. "This time I'll throw a pebble. Grab it in your talons and don't drop it! Go!"

Back raced Eagle. His sharp eyes straining ahead to see the pebble. He did see the Whizenhunnt make a throwing motion, but it was too much for his brain to compute at that speed. Again, and again, and again they tried. Sometimes the kelp, sometimes the pebble. Eagle was exhausted, and he was hungry, but the Whizenhunnt insisted he keep trying.

'Fly faster, clear your mind, let it come to you,' he grumbled in his head. 'Blah, blah, blah, blah.' He was so tired, but he had to keep trying. He really did want super vision. Maybe that's why this was so hard, because he wanted it so bad. Papa Numa had said that if you hang onto something too tightly, you might squeeze the life out of it. Well okay then, here we go again. There's Whizenhunnt. Pretend she's the kelp. He smiled. Clear mind, swim fast, find kelp, see kelp, attack kelp, go home!

Off Eagle went like a flash, eating up the meters with every stroke of his powerful wings. The Whizenhunnt threw the kelp up into the current. He felt calm and relaxed; To tired to think about missing, or think much at all. He exhaled slowly. Then... There it was! Riding up into the current, spinning, hesitating, dashing off again. Somehow, everything seemed to be moving so slow; he could see the torn edges of the kelp fluttering in the current. It danced and swooped closer. His legs reached out casually and he saw the kelp explode into pieces as his talons passed through. Suddenly he was a hundred yards past the Whizenhunnt.

"Oh yeah!" he screamed. "I did it! Did you see that?"

"Stop celebrating and go again! A pebble this time!"

Was she serious!?

"Go!" she yelled.

"Who needs sleep!" he yelled. "I can do this!"

Again and again they tried, but he missed every time and the light was falling fast. Finally it was truly too dark, and he thought for sure they would be heading back to Papa Numa's very soon. But when he mentioned this, the Whizenhunnt said, "Oh no, Mr Eagle, this is where we sleep tonight. Cuddled down into the soft mud. It makes a comfy bed."

Narwhal and Turtle were excited about the errand Papa Numa had sent them on.

"I've never been there before," said Narwhal. "What's it like?"

"It's sooo cool," said Turtle. "There are so many colors, and sounds, and streets. Huge buildings, and cars, and people everywhere. All different kinds of people. Everyone has their own language. I got lost one time. Got sucked down a dark alley by a bad current and ended up in a pile of trash with some creepy Angler fish glowing their lights in my eyes. I've never been so scared in my life, but Papa Numa found me and ran off the Anglers."

"It sounds scary," said Narwhal.

They were on their way to the Trunkline Current, which would take them around the mountain, and across The Great Valley to that wonderful city nestled up in The Further Hills, Oceanopolis.

ᘛᘛᘛᘛᘛᘛ

Eagle spent a long and exhausting week with the Whizenhunnt. There were long spells where he sat and worked on quietening the mind, staying with the breath, slowing the randon thought chatter, followed by intense physical activity charged with mental focus.

The amazing thing was how much better he was getting. His senses were quickening. He had better control over fine movements and hand-eye coordination. On his third day, he shredded the kelp five times.

The Whisenhunnt mixed things up sometimes. She would disappear into the trenches and he would have to locate her in mid swim by listening for a whistling sound she would make, then redirect and see the kelp, all at super-high speeds. It was getting impossibly hard.

This was the most physically and mentally exhausted he had ever been. In fact, he was getting upset at how hard he was being pushed. Because he was upset, he did worse, which made him outright mad. The Whizenhunnt told him in smug tones, "I'd be happy to take you back up to the surface and send you off to your feathered folk if this is too hard for you."

"No!" cried Eagle. Somehow, when she said this, he was able to redirect his anger into an intense determination to succeed. "I can take anything you throw at me! Let's go again!"

Yes, this was hard beyond words. It was a new frontier, but a frontier he would conquer!

∾∾∾∾∾∾∾

Oceanopolis had a way of filtering the light. It looked as if it were jumping through crystals. Swirling rainbows sparkled on every surface. Magnificent towers with granite buttresses and marble casements lined the wide street. A row of giant frond trees grew down the center of the street. They were on the Boulevard of Palaces which leads up to the Halls of Legislation, those great institutions were the most serious questions are pondered. Beyond, there were sprawling neighborhoods built of less impressive materials. Areas of industry where imports and exports were processed by processing officials. There were schools and universities with libraries and theaters, plus Departments of Divinity with tall temples and domed churches.

The kaleidoscope of colors and creatures and languages kept Narwhal's mind in a whirl, and his eyes and his ears in a constant swirl. Turtle chattered happily as they went along, but Narwhal didn't hear any of it. Turtle's voice blended in with the other voices and sounds, and the sounds bled into the colors and lights, reflecting around on all the structures and shapes his delighted eyes found.

Turtle had the address that Papa Numa had given them, but he had to stop and asked directions a couple times. At last they found themselves ducking under an arch into a quiet and simple courtyard. In the corner, next to a door, and under the eaves of the overhanging roof, sat an old man on a three-legged stool. Both his hands rested on his cane, both eyes quietly watched Narwhal and Turtle as they walked his way. He didn't say a word, but his eyes weren't unkind.

"Excuse me Sir," said Turtle." We come from Papa Numa. He said we'd find a letter here, to bring it back to him."

The old man got up from his stool and motioned for them to wait. He went inside and was gone for a long time. Finally he came back out, sat down on his stool, and with a motion, invited them through the door.

Inside they found themselves in a small room, bare of furnishings. There was another door though, so they went through it and continued down a short hallway. At the end there was another door, and a three-legged stool with an old man with both hands on his cane, watching them quietly.

"Um..." said Turtle. He glanced at Narwhal uncertainly. "We're here for a letter for Papa Numa?"

The old man motioned for them to wait, and went quietly through the door. After a long while, he came back and motioned them through.

They found a stairway that went down, down, down, winding left and right and then down some more, until it came out into an empty room with one other door and a three-legged stool. On the stool there were two letters and a note. The note said, 'Take both letters and go through the second door.'

Narwhal and Turtle looked at one another. There was only one thing to do. Turtle picked up the two letters, Narwhal opened the door, and they both stepped through into a small, tight space that barely had enough room for both of them. They squeezed in.

"This is weird!" whispered Narwhal.

"I know!" said Turtle.

"I'm having a hard time breathing!" said Narwhal. "You have the letters?"

"Yes," said Turtle. "What should we do now?"

"Maybe we should close the door." Narwhal wriggled himself around to where he could reach the doorknob with his fin, and pulled it closed. It was completely dark and quiet.

All of a sudden, there was a loud bang, and they felt the tiny room give a jolt. It seemed to be moving upwards. Nice mellow music started playing from above their heads, and then there was a ding. The little room stopped moving and the door opened.

They found themselves squeezed into a phone booth on Ceremonial Parkway. The crowds were hurrying and bustling all around them. The air was full to bursting with the busy importance of everything. Narwhal look down and saw the two letters in Turtle's hand.

"That was so weird! Are both letters for Papa Numa? I wonder who those weird men were. Were they twins or the same person?"

"Yep, Oceanopolis can be a weird place," said Turtle as he looked at the letters. "This one is for Papa Numa, and this one... Wow!..."

"What!? Tell me!" said Narwhal.

"It's to King Brighton!" said Turtle.

So... Narwhal and Turtle headed back on the long journey home to deliver their letters. They took The Undercurrent over to Main Current South. Got off at Pickle Heaven Avenue, and went through Magic Canyon which came out on the other side of the mountain where they caught the Trunkline Current for the long swim home. Back to the Palace of King Brighton. Back to Papa Numa's village and his Coral Tree. They decided that Turtle would take the letter to the king, and Narwhal would go straight to Papa Numa's.

So that's what they did.

〰〰〰〰〰〰

When Eagle got back to Papa Numa's he was so tired that he didn't think to ask about Narwhal and Turtle. He ate several sea cucumbers and fell fast asleep. When he awoke, Narwhal was there. He told Eagle all about their trip to Oceanopolis. It sounded amazing. Eagle wished like everything he had gone too.

He tried to tell Narwhal about his week, but it was hard to explain Super Vision. "Seeing with your eyes, but also with your mind. But you can't think about it or it doesn't work. And the Whizenhunnt was no fun at all. It was just push, push, push, the whole time. But I can see faster now... or slower. It's hard to know which." Later, he spent some time napping with Papa Numa under the

Coral Tree, and talking about his time with the Whizenhunnt. He told Papa Numa that he wished he had gone to Oceanopolis with Narwhal and Turtle instead of hanging out with her. He could have had a torture week any ol' time.

Papa Numa said, "I understand. You had a tough week, and your friends were off on a big adventure to the biggest city in the world. I don't blame you for wishing you had been there. But don't forget that your time was well spent. What you learned with the Whizenhunnt was much more valuable then a sightseeing trip. In fact, from now on you'll be able to appreciate traveling more fully since you're able to see with Super Vision."

"I know," said Eagle. "But I'm still sad I didn't get to see Oceanopolis. I may never get another chance! Oooooh I wish, wish, wish I had gone to Oceanopolis! I know what you said is true, but I still wish I had gone! That's a chance I'll never have again and it just breaks my heart!" wailed poor Eagle.

"I have a secret for you," said Papa Numa. "It's so simple you might miss it if you don't use your Super Vision!" He smiled. "The reason why people are unhappy is because they wish that their life was different in some way."

"What do you mean?" asked Eagle. "I love my life!"

"Well, I'm glad to hear that. But you were just now wishing that you had gone with your friends to the city instead of training with Whizenhunnt. That's wishing for your life to be different than it is, and it's making you unhappy. There's no point in being sad over something in the past that you can never change. You may as well be happy about what did happen, for how much more skillful you are. You see, the number one cause of happiness is gratitude. That's where you always find joy, even in unhappy situations. There's always something to be grateful for, and if you choose to focus on that, you'll always be able to find the happiness. Aaah, here's Turtle. Hello lad. Wonderful timing. Would you mind finding Narwhal and rejoining us here? Then you can tell us all about your adventure."

Before too long Turtle and Narwhal were sitting with Eagle and Papa Numa. Turtle told them all about delivering the letter to the penguin king. He said the King was very dramatic and fainted three times when he read the letter. Papa Numa nodded his head as if this made sense. In the show of gratitude to Turtle for delivering the letter, the king had given Turtle a pair of season tickets to The

Gaming Grounds. Prime seats, 3rd row, center left. Papa Numa sighed, and then nodded as if this too made sense.

"Oh Grandpa, I almost forgot!" said Turtle. "The king asked for you to go see him tomorrow." Papa Numa nodded.

Suddenly the Whizenhunnt dropped into the middle of the small gathering, floating down from above. She leaned towards Papa Numa and said in a loud whisper, "You should take the feathered one with you." Papa Numa nodded his head.

Apparently she had been listening in from the boughs of the Coral Tree! Eagle wondered how long she'd been there.

Turtle jumped .up and said, "Turtle too! I want to go!"

Papa Numa nodded his head, "Yes, and you too Narwhal." he said.

"I'll be up here," said the Whizenhunnt. She jetted upwards and disappeared into the Coral Tree.

"What does your letter say Grandpa?" asked Turtle.

Papa Numa nodded his head. "Tonight we sleep, and dream, and sleep; and with the dawn we'll find the king and then the time for letters. Off to bed with you now."

Chapter Three
Giants Are Coming!

Eagle sat in silent amazement next to Narwhal and Turtle. This wasn't the throne room or The Gaming Grounds, but a private council chamber. King Brighton was pacing up and down, shaking the letter over his head, saying, "This is a disaster! What, oh what, oh what! are we going to do!?" he wailed.

Papa Numa was there as well as several other important advisers. It turned out that Papa Numa was, in fact, an important adviser.

One of the squid advisers said, "I think we should muster the troops your majesty! Call up the reserves! Ring the town bells! Declare a national emergency!"

Another said, "Or what about this! Maybe we should just carry on and pretend we didn't get our mail?"

"I don't think so!" cried the king. "Doing nothing is a terrible idea! Terrible, TERRIBLE!! What say you Papa Numa?"

"Indeed, it is a difficult question," said Papa Numa. "A middle course is usually prudent. I recommend you issue a Classified Notice of Imminent Potential Muster to the troops. Also, it would be helpful to know more about the quantity and qualities of these giants before they arrive."

"That's all well and good if it can be done." said the king. "But how is beyond me!"

"Well, I happen to have a young friend who has been training for just this type of mission. He's very fast and his vision is exceptional."

"Stop! Stop! Stop!" said the king. "Let me guess! You're talking about Eagle, right!?"

"Yes, that's right," said Papa Numa.

"I knew it!" said the king. "What do you say Eagle? Are you ready for a close-up, fly-by look at these giants?"

Eagle was stunned. He had not been expecting this and could only nod his head, 'Yes.'

"It's settled then!" cried the king. "You'll be the first to see the dreaded giants! Get a good look, then come back and tell us all about it! This is so exciting!"

"What are the giants like?" whispered Eagle to Narwhal. He was getting a bad feeling.

"They're the huge monsters from the old stories," whispered Narwhal. "So big they could swallow me whole. Some people say they're not real. Just old legends, fairy tales."

"Yeah, They're huge! I've never seen one though," said Turtle with a frown. "They never come here. Thank goodness the letters warned us! It looks bad."

King Brighton called Eagle to the front of the throne room and stood up on his throne. He declaimed his gratitude to Eagle for volunteering for such a dangerous mission. Selflessly sacrificing himself for the good of the kingdom... You'd think he had been reading Cicero.

Papa Numa whispered to the king that maybe time was of the essence.

"Right you are!" said the king. "Off you go Eagle! May vigilance float at your side!"

ᘒᘒᘒᘒᘒᘒ

Papa Numa took Eagle, Narwhal and Turtle out to the edge of The Abysmal Drop.

"This is where we must leave you, Eagle. Or rather, where you must leave us," said Papa Numa. "If our messenger informs us correctly, they should be coming from that direction." He pointed. "Swim your fastest, and when you find them, get a good look, but don't slow down. Use your Super Vision. One pass on the way out, and one on the way back. Hopefully they won't even know you're there."

"How will I know what they are?" asked Eagle.

"Don't worry about that. You'll know," said Papa Numa. "For one thing, it's their huge size. Too big to miss. Also, they constantly dive from the surface back down into the deep, and then up again. From what I've learned I'm guessing it's in part for them to breathe, and in part for them to eat. Regardless, it is a regular habit of theirs. Just look for something big going up or down. Off you go now. You'll be fine."

Eagle took a deep breath, said goodbye to his friends, and shot off through the water like a dart. In a blink he was gone from sight.

"I hope he'll be okay," said Narwhal.

"Me too," said Turtle.

"It's true, there are dangers," said Papa Numa, "but Eagle has a strong mind, as you can see from the luster of his air suit, and that's the first requirement for overcoming obstacles, a strong mind. You boys stay here and keep an eye out for him. I expect he'll be back in a few hours."

ଓଓଓଓଓଓଓ

Eagle flew out over The Abysmal Drop. He knew there must be a bottom down there somewhere, but it was deeper than he could go and it made him feel vulnerable. A dark unfathomable abyss snapping at his feet. He wondered what kind of monsters were down there, and would they come up from the depths to eat him. Eagle worked hard to clear his mind and focus on his mission. Don't let the random thoughts take over.

Eagle was flying at breathtaking speeds, his head on a swivel, searching for any sign of movement. Many times he saw smaller fish and other creatures but nothing that matched the descriptions of the giants. He had been swimming for a long time now, and the light was slowly draining off when Eagle heard a rumbling, trumpeting sound. He stopped and looked around, holding his breath, straining his eyes. Suddenly, shooting up past him, erupting from below, rushed a mighty creature, jostling him about like a cork in a typhoon.

Eagle screamed. He was being spun around by the turbulent water. It roared and rushed and slammed him back and forth. The giant crashed back into the water, and he was dashed about again for several terrifying moments. When he finally got his bearings, he found himself surrounded by swarms of what seem to be tiny lobster. They said their name was Krill and they were trying to escape the

45

Leviathan. He wished them good luck with that. What he assumed was a giant was now some distance away, and Eagle needed to hurry to get a good look.

He was able to capture all the emotions and thoughts flooding through his mind, saying hi to each one, and putting it on a mental shelf for later discussion. Then he gave all his attention to his eyes, and saw many details with his super vision. He saw the giant clearly as it dove again. It was a mighty fish-like creature with grayish leathery skin, no scales. It had fins as big as Narwhal, and a thickly muscled tail that could surely destroy Papa Numa's entire village in one sweep. It's head was built like a battering ram that hinged opened into a mouth that could swallow a small ship. It was a terrifying sight; a mountain of flesh crashing through the water. He felt so tiny.

Eagle suddenly realized that there was probably more than one giant out here! He could still be in danger! For several panic stricken moments he spun in circles like a top, looking up and down and all around, his heart thundering in his chest and ears.

No, he didn't see any more, thank goodness. Only now, he couldn't see the first one either! It was gone, and he was so thoroughly disoriented after spinning in circles that he had no idea which way to go. Eagle was trying hard not to panic. He wasn't sure which way back to Papa Numa and Narwhal and Turtle. He wouldn't be able to complete his mission for King Brighton, and it was almost dark! It was so scary! Eagle focused on taking deep slow breaths like Papa Numa had taught him. It helped him stay calm. He was going to have to think his way out of this.

Eagle thought and thought, and as he sat there pondering fearfully, the light grew dimmer and trailed off to barely a faint glow. Eagle knew that of all the directions he could go, only one would be right. It was a hard decision.

At that moment, Krill began sweeping past. Eagle called out to them. "Krill! Stop! Can you help me please? I'm lost and don't know which way to go!"

Krill stopped swimming and gathered round Eagle. They surrounded him as if he was inside a ball made up of tiny lobster. "We'll help you if you promise not to eat us," they said. Eagle agreed.

"Can tell me which way the giant went? I need to follow it. And I need to reach The Coral Ridge"

"What's this giant you speak of?" asked Krill.

"You know!" said Eagle. "That huge creature with the massive tail that almost ate us earlier!"

"Oh goodness gracious!" exclaimed Krill. "You're talking about the Leviathan! We recommend you stay as far away as possible from those! Very dangerous! Entire civilizations of our Krill ancestors have disappeared in one pass of the Leviathan."

"I'm terribly sorry," said Eagle. "I wish that hadn't happened, but I really need to know which way it went! I'm trying to help make sure my friends don't get eaten too!"

Krill held a whispering conversation. They seemed to come to some conclusion and said to him, "Okay, if you must go, you should head that way."

Krill realigned themselves into a long arrow showing Eagle the direction he should travel. Eagle said, "Thank you very much! I really must be off now! it's getting dark!"

Krill became a hand, and waved to him, saying, "I've never seen one of those before, but I hope it survives. Where those feathers it was wearing? Add that to the database."

Eagle was off in the direction indicated. It was so dark that he was flying pretty well blind. It was thanks to his super vision that he was able to see at all. He was going so fast though, that he didn't see the giant tale sweeping through the water until he swam smack into it. It felt like a house had hit him. All the air was knocked from his lungs and his head was clanging like a thousand bells. He reeled backwards through the water, gasping for breathe.

Eagle, tumbling through the water, didn't see the Leviathan spinning around. It wasn't used to getting attacked by small creatures from behind. Eagle found himself eye to eye with the gargantuan, enormous, and entirely terrifying giant. He hung suspended in the dark water, the giant eyeball stared at him from the towering wall of wrinkled flesh surrounding it.

Eagle was terrified, and yet mesmerized. In the darkness, it seemed that the universe had disappeared, and the only thing left was himself, this eye, and the space between them. He didn't know how long they hung suspended in silence. It could have been a moment, or several hours.

In a fit of instinct, Eagle made a dash for it. He knew in the back of his mind that he could swim faster than the giant from a complete stop, and it was pointing the wrong way, but he had only one chance. He had never swam so fast. He swam like certain death was on his very heels. He swam until he felt his heart and lungs exploding, and only then did he look around and start to slow when he saw nothing behind him.

He kept moving at a fast clip. All the while it was getting lighter and lighter. It was beautiful the way the morning sun dropped a filtered filigree of sparkling crystals that danced through the water. In this emerging light of day, Eagle saw Narwhal and Turtle, and the towering cliffs rising up from the depths of The Abysmal Drop. He had made it! By some miracle!

Turtle and Narwhal were sleeping. Eagle flew in so fast that he almost skidded into Narwhal. Between trying to catch his breath, he yelled, "Wake up! Wake up! Where's Papa Numa and the king? We have to find them! Fast! The Giant is coming!"

Narwhal and Turtle woke up with a start. "Aaah!" screamed Narwhal.

"Eeek!" shrieked Turtle.

"Hurry!" yelled Eagle. "I found the Leviathan. It almost ate me!"

Narwhal and Turtle looked at one another. "What's a Leviathan?" asked Turtle."

"The giant!" cried Eagle. "Krill called it a Leviathan. Come on! We have to go!"

"Oh goodness!" said Narwhal, and they all raced off for Papa Numa and the King.

〜〜〜〜〜〜

"I don't know how much time we have before the Giant gets here," Eagle told the king. "It was dark most of the time while I was escaping, and it's hard to judge time and distance while running for your life! I do know that the creature is fast. As fast as it is vast. Krill said it devastates entire civilizations!"

"Krill!" said the king with a dismissive toss of his head, "I know those little critters. So small you can hardly see them. What could they possibly know about civilizations. What say you Papa Numa?"

"I know nothing of the Leviathan this Krill speaks of, but according to Eagle's description, it is indeed one of the giants. I'm surprised there's not more of them. They've always been shrouded in mystery; where they come from, where they go, what is their purpose. Why do they now seek us out? It may not be a bad idea to wait on the lip of The Abysmal Drop in case talking is an option when the giant arrives."

The king thought this was a great idea. He recommended Papa Numa and Eagle be his representatives. If the giant is aggressive, he reasoned to himself, Eagle would be fast enough to get away and report back so he could escape, and hopefully Papa Numa's shell would be hard enough to protect him if it comes to that.

Papa Numa agreed that this was a good course of action. Eagle was wishing for some other course, but he acted confident because he didn't want to let Papa Numa down. Anything that didn't put him face-to-face with the Leviathan again!

"I'll be fine!" he told himself. "All my training is going to make the difference. I'm the only feathered upper-worlder with an awesome air suit that's explored the ocean floor and can help save the kingdom! Plus, I'm the only one with personal experience of the Leviathan." Despite trying to cheer himself up with these words, there was still a dark terror that hung within his chest and floated behind his eyeballs.

Narwhal and Turtle decided to go to the edge of The Abysmal Drop with them. Papa Numa and Eagle continued out into the open water several hundred yards. They hadn't been there very long when in the distance they could see a dark spot in the water, growing larger and larger as it dove up and down through the water.

Papa Numa started swimming in circles, waving his arms. "You too!" he said to Eagle. "Swim around and make some noise. We need to get it's attention."

Eagles swallowed, but did like Papa Numa asked. He sped backwards and forwards, up and down, in big circles, and twirled round upside down, yelling, "Stop! Stop! Stop! Let's talk! Talk! Talk!"

The giant seemed to be slowing down, but it slid past Papa Numa, nearly catching him with a 12-foot fin. The swirling eddies spun the old turtle in circles, and with a swish of the giant tail, Papa Numa disappeared into the dark depths.

Eagle was frantic. Papa Numa was gone! The shelf of The Abysmal Drop was getting closer and closer. Eagle was waving his wings, and yelling, "Stop Please! Oh Please Please Please Stop!"

Then things went even more wrong. Maybe a current had taken him, or the creature had sped up, but the Leviathan slammed into Eagle with its nose, battering him along in front of it.

Narwhal saw the giant coming towards them, and he saw that Eagle was in trouble. It was a fight that Eagle could never win! Without thinking, Narwhal dashed off through the water yelling, "Leave my friend alone! Don't you dare hurt him! I'm coming, Eagle!"

The giant was opening its mouth, and Narwhal was sure that Eagle was about to be eaten! He dashed forward with his unicorn nose as fast has he could go, and stabbed with all his might into the Leviathan's nose. The giant lurched and rolled in the water, turning sideways, and came to rest with a bump along the edge of The Abysmal Drop like a ship docking at a wharf. Eagle and Narwhal landed with a thump next to Turtle. Once again Eagle found himself uncomfortably close to that massive eye.

"Hi! Sorry about that!" said a cheerful voice. "I was trying to stop, but it takes me awhile sometimes." She laughed. "I tried to tell you but then your friend stabbed me. That really hurt!"

Turtle laughed in relief and said, "Hi!" Eagle and Narwhal sat in stunned silence, looking at the huge form floating there off the shelf. Just then Papa Numa came swimming up over the edge.

"Awe, good," he said. "I see we all survived. Hello to you, my giant friend, if friend indeed you be. I am Papa Numa, adviser to King Brighton. At Your Service." Eagle was so relieved to see Papa Numa!

"Greetings, Papa Numa. My name is Dodona. I have been sent by my king, King of Leviathia, King Pompilius, to inquire about an Upper World eagle said to be residing in these lands." She looked at Eagle as she said this. "I believe we've

already met, but under very different circumstances. I couldn't be sure in the dark. Hello Eagle," she said.

Eagle waved an air suit clad wing. Her voice, strangely, reminded Eagle of his mother's voice. He felt overwhelmed, and suddenly home sick. He would give anything to be with his mom right now, curled up under her warm wing. "Um... Hi," He said.

"It's nice to meet you," said Dodona.

"Thanks," he said.

Papa Numa interjected, suggesting they all move to the palace lawns where they could introduce Dodona to King Brighton whose ears were the intended target of any messages from the Leviathan king. He commended Dodona on her impressive water displacement and wondered if she were a delicate swimmer. "It would be unfortunate if the fragile architecture of the coral castles were damaged," he diplomatically noted.

Dodona smiled and said, "I completely understand. But don't worry, I can maneuver with the most delicate finesse."

ꙮꙮꙮꙮꙮꙮ

So the five made their way to King Brighton's Palace. Four small creatures, flanked and overshadowed by the slowly swimming bulk of a ninety three foot long blue whale. Papa Numa was distinctly aware of the destructive capabilities of such a large mammal, but he didn't sense any ill intentions from Dodona.

When they arrived at the palace, they really caused a stir. If anyone had ever seen a blue whale, it was in the open sea, and no one ever went there. It was as if a creature of Legend and myth, and as big as a mountain, had shown up on the palace lawns.

Papa Numa talked with the king for a long time before the king would come out. He was certain it would be better for Papa Numa to mediate, but Papa Numa insisted. "Kings must be kingly sometimes," he said with a smile.

So the king came out his palace flanked by two dozen walrus led by Horace. Papa Numa came behind with the squad of squid advisers. All around, curious

bystanders were gathering. Word spread fast, and people from the surrounding slopes and villages were already filtering into the crowd. Eagle saw the Whizenhunnt. He hadn't seen her since that day at Papa Numa's Coral Tree.

Horace introduced the king in a rumbling, trumpeting voice: "HEAR YE, HEAR YE, WILL YOU PUT YOUR HANDS TOGETHER FOR THE CONQUEROR OF GALAXIES; THE MOST HEAVENLY AND WISE AND GLORIOUS RULER, WHO MEASURES NOT IN INCHES, BUT IN KINGLY KINGLINESS... GIVE IT UP FOR KIIIINNGG BRIGHTONNN PARTHOLONNNN!!! (that's his full name.)"

When the cheering petered out, Dodona said, "Greetings, King Brighton. My name is Dodona. I've been sent by my king, the Leviathan king, King Pompilius, to inquire after the Upper World eagle said to be residing in these lands."

"Oh?" said the king in a strained voice.

"Thank you for coming to talk to me, King Brighton."

"You're welcome," said the king, looking up, and up, and up, at the unbelievably massive creature before him. He was in awe. Speechless.

"King Pompilius was told a marvelous tale," said Dodona, "of a feathered creature come down from The Upper World, living in the lands of The Coral Ridge." The king nodded his head, still speechless. Dodona continued. "I've been sent to look into the truth of this tale, and imagine my surprise, on discovering my prize, there before my very eyes, as I landed on The Coral Shore."

Papa Numa tilted his wrinkled forehead. "I wonder, Dodona, who told your King this wonderful tale."

"I've wondered that myself," said Dodona. "Rumor has an opinion that the news came from the King's chief adviser, the Whizenhunnt Okon-o-tin'hoo."

Everything went quiet. All the eyes so far fastened on Dodona slowly swiveled around and fastened on the Whizenhunnt.

"What!?" she asked.

Here the king found his voice. He cleared his throat, and stood up as tall as he could, looking up, and up at Dodona. "Whizenhunnt's are not what you came here to discuss I'm sure. You've already met Eagle it seems. He is my loyal subject. I would like to know," continued King Brighton, "what is the full intent of your mission from King Pompilius."

"I'm glad you asked, King Brighton," said Dodona. "My instructions were to carry nothing further than to inquire if Eagle of The Upper World would honor King Pompilius with a visit to his Royal Court. My king is exceedingly desirous to make this unique personage's acquaintance." Turning to Eagle she said, "Eagle, would you come visit my home and meet King Pompilius?"

King Brighton spoke up before Eagle could reply. "It's absolutely imperative that I speak with my advisors in private before you receive an answer! Eagle, would you please join us in the throne room? Dodona, you are welcome to stay in the palace lawns, but if you are more comfortable beyond The Abysmal Drop, please don't hesitate to wait for us there. Good day Madam!"

The king appeared to be extremely agitated. His voice was shaking and he gesticulated wildly with his flippers. "Horace, disperse the crowds!" he yelled over his shoulder as he headed for the palace. Papa Numa motioned for Eagle and the others to come as well.

◈◈◈◈◈◈

The mood in the throne room was tense. King Brighton paced up and down on his throne dais. Papa Numa and several advisers ranged around the king with Eagle and his friends off to one side in a small group.

"This is crazy!" whispered Eagle. "I don't know what everybody is thinking, but I'm hungry! I haven't had anything to eat since Dodona almost ate me with Krill!"

"It's a good thing she's friendly!" said Turtle. "She's big enough to eat us all if she wanted!"

"I thought you were a goner for sure when she swam up on you at The Abysmal Drop!" said Narwhal.

At the front of the throne room, the king was exclaiming, "I won't have it! I won't let them take away my best warrior, even if he's still in training!" Papa Numa was trying to say something but the king wasn't listening. "They can't just come in here and demand a visit from him anytime they want! It's not fair!" Eagle started to pay attention. It was him they were talking about after all.

Papa Numa said, "Please be calm king. They haven't asked anything unreasonable. Eagle is after all, a highly unusual visitor in these parts."

"And that's exactly why it's so unacceptable!" yelled the king. "I won't allow him to go! He came here first! He's our unusual visitor, not theirs!"

"Excuse me, King," said Eagle. "But like Papa Numa said, I am visitor. I don't remember signing any contracts making me a citizen and subject." He looked at Papa Numa uncertainly.

"You're entirely right lad," said Papa Numa. "You're from a whole different world, and while the universal laws apply to us all, no matter where we're from, our local laws and edicts have no power to restrain you unless you are in violation of them, which you are not. That means, you can visit whomever you please."

"You can't tell him that!" yelled the king. "I insist you tell him the opposite of what you just said!"

"I'm sorry, King Brighton," said Papa Numa, "but I'm bound to tell the truth and to honestly advise those who honestly seek."

You could see that King Brighton knew Papa Numa was right, but he was still angry. "Horace!" he screamed. "Get in here! I need to bellow in rage!" Horace came through the door as quickly as his giant bulk allowed him. The king's tiny scream was quickly drowned out by Horace's earth-shattering, bone wrenching roar. Horace's head was thrown back, his great flippers braced, and his tail arched up with the effort. Even the king had to cover his ears.

When the roar finally stopped bouncing around the room, the king smiled and said, "Ahhhh, that feels better. Thanks, Horace. Okay, Eagle." He said, riveting Eagle with a steely glare, "You know I want you to stay, but what is it that you want?"

Eagle thought about it for a minute, slowly realizing how homesick he was. Tears welled up in his eyes as he thought about his mountains, the wind, tree trees, and his mom and dad, brothers and sister. "I want to go home," he said to the king in the choked up voice. "Back to The Upper World. I like it here and I want to stay, but I'm homesick and I want to see my family."

The king nodded his head, closed his eyes and sighed. Eagle turned to the Whizenhunnt and asked her, "If I go back to The Upper World, will I ever be able to come back?"

Everyone was looking at the Whizenhunnt. She narrowed her eyes. "That's a complicated question," she said. "The short answer is that you can come back if you know where to find a Whizenhunnt who knows the secrets for binding the air suit and is willing to do it for you."

"Are there many who know that trick?" asked Eagle.

"There are many Whizenhunnts, but few know the binding process."

Eagle was silent for a moment, then he went to Narwhal and asked, "What should I do?"

"I don't know," Narwhal said. "I don't want you to leave. I like having you for a friend, but if you need to go, I understand. Maybe you should ask Papa Numa."

"That's a good idea," said Eagle. "Thanks. You're a good friend too."

When they were all leaving the throne room, the king called for the Whizenhunnt to stay behind. "I have some questions for you," he said. "I'm curious how King Pompilius' advisor, Okon-o-tin'hoo, knew about Eagle." Eagle didn't hear her answer.

The next day he and Papa Numa told Dodona that he would like to visit King Pompilius as soon as he could, but first he needed to take a trip home. Dodona said she would be more than happy to wait as long as he needed. She could then escort him back to her kingdom.

They also had a long visit with King Brighton. Eagle told him that he did like The Coral Ridge very much, and that he wanted to be helpful in any way possible. They agreed that after Eagle visited The Upper World, he would come back for a short visit before heading off to King Pompilius' Court. The king would send a letter with Eagle for King Pompilius.

After some gentle persuasion from Papa Numa, The Whizenhunnt agreed to help Eagle exit and re-enter the ocean. They set the date for sunrise, at the island where he had first entered the water. He would be gone forty-nine hours, then back into his air suit and off to Leviathia.

Made in United States
Troutdale, OR
11/25/2024

25265276R00043